STAR TALES

North American Indian Stories about the Stars

Retold by
Gretchen Will Mayo

Illustrated by
Gretchen Will Mayo

WALKER AND COMPANY
NEW YORK

First published in the United States of America in 1987 by the
Walker Publishing Company, Inc.

Published simultaneously in Canada by John Wiley & Sons
Canada, Limited, Rexdale, Ontario.

Book design by Laurie McBarnette

Library of Congress Cataloging-in-Publication Data

Mayo, Gretchen.
Star tales.

Includes index.
Summary: A collection of Indian legends about the
stars, moon, and nighttime sky.
1. Indians of North America—Legends. 2. Stars—
Folklore. [1. Indians of North America—Legends.
2. Stars—Folklore. 3. Moon—Folklore] I. Title.
E98.F6M35   1987   398.2'6'08997   86-23360
ISBN 0-8027-6672-2
ISBN 0-8027-6673-0 (lib. bdg.)

Printed in the United States of America

10 9 8 7 6 5 4 3 2 1

For Tom,
Meg, Molly and Ann

My appreciation and thanks
to Dr. Alice B. Kehoe
and
the Milwaukee Public Museum

For all of the reading STARS
who
open this book

Gretchen Will Mayo
10/2001

CONTENTS

INTRODUCTION

Leaning close to a glowing campfire, a gathering of young people watch The Old One as he acts out a story. His wrinkled hands stroke the night air. He is describing Crane Woman's escape from her earthly husband, the greedy and evil Wolf Man. Crane Woman and her two starving sons have nowhere else to run from the wicked Wolf Man, but they find safety in the sky where they will become stars.

The young people are Native American Indians. The stories might have been told last night or a hundred years ago, for the tale of Crane Woman is an ancient one. Native American Indians have spun tales for one another for century upon century. Their stories reflect their ways of life, their beliefs, and the laws of their tribes.

Some of the storytellers were farmers. They told tales of Corn Maiden. Other Indians roamed the plains, hunting buffalo. From their tribes came stories of ghostly buffalo herds. There were whalers and salmon fishermen, trappers and shepherds, basket weavers and potters. The countless ancient Indian tribes were as different as the land was different across the continent, but they all shared a love for storytelling.

Native American ancestors were keenly aware of the land and the sky that surrounded them. They felt that all creation was connected. They believed that spirits could appear in all things, from rocks to ravens to falling stars. When they looked at the night sky, they joined all the world's people in imagining what the stars could be. They wove many tales about the sky country.

The gifted Indian tale-spinners have passed along the thread of their Native American stories from generation to generation. Sometimes they have reverently conformed to the original myths. Often they embellished the tales with details springing from their own imaginations. The stories in this collection are another link in that creative storytelling tradition and are offered with a sense of appreciation for what has been told before.

STAR TALES

Coyote Makes the Constellations

Some Native American ancestors looked at the night sky and saw the outlines of familiar animals dotted by stars. Other Indians, though, imagined that each individual star was a person, animal, or object in the sky country.

The Wasco Indians told a tale to explain how these star "pictures" appeared in the sky. The Wascos were part of the Chinook tribe which lived on the southern shores of the Columbia River in Oregon.

Coyote is a trickster and one of their legendary heroes. Although he is an animal, Coyote talks and behaves like a human. His many tricks confuse and frustrate the people but, when it is convenient, he also gives them gifts. He has powers greater than any human, and he likes to be admired. Even though Coyote is not to be trusted, the Indians often benefit from his antics in their tales.

COYOTE MAKES THE CONSTELLATIONS

One night, Coyote was making his way through the fields when he came upon five wolf brothers. They were seated with their dog, looking at the sky.

"Why do you sit and look above?" asked Coyote.

"It's no business of yours," answered one of the wolves.

"Such unpleasant fellows," thought Coyote to himself. He sat down beside them anyway. The wolf brothers paid no attention, but continued to gaze at the sky.

"What is it you see up there?" inquired Coyote after a time.

"Nothing!" snapped the wolf brothers. Still they stared at the stars. Long minutes passed. No one made a move.

"Well, I see you have truly lost your wits," muttered Coyote, and he got up to leave.

"If you must know," growled the oldest wolf, "we see a bear up there, and we are watching it." Coyote sat down and looked again. Sure enough, he saw among the stars the outline of a large bear.

Finally, Coyote said, "Let's all go up and take a close look at that bear."

"How can we do that?" scowled the wolves.

"First I will shoot that small star with my bow and arrows," boasted Coyote. The others laughed as he shot his first arrow, but they could not see it come down again. Coyote shot another arrow, and then another. Now the laughing stopped. All the star-watchers saw a chain of arrows hanging from the sky. Coyote continued to shoot his arrows, and soon the chain reached the place where they were sitting.

"Now we can go see that bear!" exclaimed Coyote. "Follow me!" And he began climbing up the arrow chain.

When all the animals had reached the sky, Coyote cautioned, "Don't get too close to the grizzly bear. You might make it angry." So each of the brothers and their dog found a place in the sky where they sat quietly and looked at the bear. The bear looked back.

Coyote looked around at the others sitting there in the sky, and he sighed. "They make such a nice picture. I'd like to keep them this way always," he said to himself. Then he thought, "If I keep the sky as it is, people below will look up and say, 'Coyote made that beautiful picture for us!'" So Coyote scampered quickly down the arrow chain, removing each of the arrows as he went.

When Coyote reached earth again, he took his arrows and disappeared over the hill. The wolf brothers and their dog still sit in the sky quietly watching the grizzly bear while the bear looks back.

Adventure Along the White River in the Sky

Today the great stroke of stars across the night sky is called the Milky Way. There once must have been almost as many different stories about the Milky Way as there were Indian tribes in North America. Some tribes believed it was the path that birds took in their migrations. The Pawnees said it was the pathway taken by spirits of the dead to the Southern Star, where they would live for eternity. The Snohomish of Puget Sound were whalers and fishermen who saw the Milky Way as a river and the scene of a conflict between the people of earth and sky.

ADVENTURE ALONG THE WHITE RIVER IN THE SKY

The Milky Way

When all the world was cold and dark, there was once a man who made canoes so tight and strong they rode the water like sleek silver fish. The canoemaker loved his work so much that he would begin every day at dawn, before the stars had left the sky, and would work late into the night. He hammered and pounded, scraped and rubbed, until his fine vessels stood worthy of the most angry waters.

Above him, in the heavens, the great chief of the sky people raged at the endless hammering. Finally, to restore silence, he sent down four of his men to capture Canoemaker.

Now across the vast land, this man alone could make such fine canoes. When the people of his village found out that he was gone, they searched everywhere for him. They looked across the frozen hills, along the streams, and even under the unfinished canoes. Finally, at the far end of the village, they found an old man who whiled away his sleepless hours looking out his window. He told them of the canoeman's capture.

The villagers wrung their hands and pulled at their hair. "What will we do without our canoemaker?" they wailed.

Amid the complaining and the crying, the old man raised his voice. "When I was a boy, storytellers said the sky could be reached by making a chain of arrows," he recalled.

The people, ready to try any means, took up their bows and set about shooting a flurry of arrows into the air. Like a cloud of mosquitoes, the arrows flew against the heavens. But not one rose high enough to stick in the sky. Robin, who had been flitting about from tree to tree, finally came forward to help them. He flew up and thrust the first arrow into the sky, then Canoemaker's people added theirs until a chain of arrows hung all the way down to the village.

Then the villagers began to climb into the heavens. They were very quiet so the great chief of the sky people would not hear them coming.

When the last of the villagers had made his way through the hole in the sky, Robin began at once to snoop around the sky country. First he found the village of the sky people along the Great White River in the Sky. Then he found the canoemaker tied to the roof of a house. After assuring the canoemaker that help was coming, Robin raced back to alert the people.

By now Robin was getting cold, but he wanted to snoop around some more. While he was shivering about the sky country, poking here, nosing there, Robin began to feel something warm and went to investigate. Along the Great White River he came upon a group of sky people gathered around a fire. Robin had no idea what this strange glowing thing was, for the lower world had never been given fire. But how he loved the warmth! "Whatever this is, we should have some of it in our village," Robin said to himself.

Cautiously, he tried to move close to the fire to take some back to earth. Each time he came near, the sky people circling the fire pushed him back into the cold. Robin was angry. He found Beaver, and they made a plan.

Beaver floated down the Great White River to the

place where the sky people were gathered around the fire. As he had expected, some of the children saw Beaver and began to chase and tease him. Beaver played their game, but managed to creep closer and closer to the fire.

Just as Beaver was able to draw up to the fire, the people from Canoemaker's village came into camp to rescue their friend. The sky people jumped with a roar and charged after them.

Beaver saw his chance and wasted no time. In the confusion, he skittered up to the fire, snatched a flaming stick, and ran off to the hole in the sky.

Meanwhile, Robin led Canoemaker's people to the rooftop where they untied their friend. They all ran along the shore of the Great White River until they reached the hole in the sky.

The chief of the sky people came thundering after them, but Canoemaker and his people made their way out of the sky and down the arrow chain safely.

Afterward, as all the village people warmed themselves around Beaver's fire, the canoemaker thanked the villagers. "I will never make the great chief of the sky people angry again," he promised. That is why Canoemaker and his people never build their canoes early in the morning or late at night.

The Race for the Prize Fish

Some of the brightest stars in the sky sparkle in the constellation that we call Orion. The Inuit of Labrador said Betelgeuse, the largest of these stars, was a bear. The three stars of Orion's belt were said to be three hunters, and the row of stars hanging below the belt was the hunter's sled.

The Indians of our Southeast said Betelgeuse was not a bear but a bee tree. The other stars were said to be three hunters who had an ax, a deerskin bag, and a ladle. They were hoping to find some honey.

The Umatilla Chinook of northeast Oregon saw something entirely different in the stars of Orion. Their star tale tells of two kinds of wind that blew through their country and a fish that was one of their favorite foods.

THE RACE FOR THE PRIZE FISH

Belt and Sword of Orion

Ever since the time that the stars were placed in the heavens, there has been a race going on among the sky people. Two canoes race, as they always have, toward a large salmon floating in a river of the sky. The three bright stars in one canoe are the Cold North Wind brothers. The three Chinook Wind brothers paddle the other canoe. They are smaller stars but they are stronger, so they are winning the race. The Cold North Wind brothers will never win because of what happened long ago to the old grandfather of Chinook Wind.

At one time, so long ago none are left who saw it, the grandfather of Chinook Wind was a fine fisherman. Although age had slowed his bones, his mind was quick and sure. So he outwitted the fish and always brought home a large catch. The old grandfather's salmon were the envy of many, but especially of Cold North Wind. He was a blustery fellow who would like to have claimed the biggest and best of the fish for himself. But Cold North Wind always came too late. Because he was fierce and accustomed to having his way, Cold North Wind began to snatch the salmon from the old man when he returned to his lodge.

Chinook Wind worried when his grandfather seemed to be doing so poorly. One day while the old man fished, Chinook Wind hid. He saw his grandfather catch many salmon. But as the old man carried his baskets to his lodge, he was stopped by Cold North Wind, who demanded the fish. Chinook Wind stepped from his hiding place.

"You can't take my grandfather's catch!" shouted Chinook Wind.

"Yes, I can, because I am stronger!" bellowed North Wind.

"There are many kinds of strength!" challenged Chinook, and the two began to wrestle.

Now Cold North Wind was of a fearsome size and powerful. He stormed and raged and threw himself about. Chinook Wind seemed little match for him. But Chinook Wind had been taught since childhood to find his own strength, and he was clever. He was also quick. Before long, Cold North Wind was huffing and puffing as Chinook slipped again and again from his grasp.

Chinook Wind won the wrestling match, and Cold North Wind lay spent at his feet. Because Chinook Wind took away some of his strength, Cold North Wind can never win the race for the prize salmon.

The Antelope Chase

The Shoshoni Indians lived along the streams in what is now Nevada, Idaho, and Utah. They constantly moved in small groups from place to place searching for food. When food was plentiful, they preserved antelope and buffalo meat for winter use. Often in the long and dreary days of winter, if the lodge held a good supply of meat, the Shoshoni passed the time singing or telling stories. They told of Giant Big Horn, the Great Brown Bear of the Mountains, of ghosts and war heroes. Someone once said, "Never were there more marvelous storytellers and never were there more willing listeners."

THE ANTELOPE CHASE

Three-Stars-in-a-Row

There were once two brothers who were hunters. These brothers spent most of their days roaming the land, hunting antelope. The wife of the older brother, who wished she could see more of the world, was always left behind to tend the camp and watch her child. The unhappy woman decided to play a trick.

One day, after the hunters had left, she put on a pair of antelope horns and wrapped herself in an antelope hide. Then she stole off to a wooded place where the brothers were hunting. When the two brothers saw the antelope horns moving among the branches, they rushed to the thicket. The antelope had disappeared. They saw only the wife, who had removed her disguise and was picking berries.

"Did you see an antelope grazing near here?" asked the brothers.

"Oh, yes! And it was a mighty one!" the wife exclaimed. "But you're too late. It ran off into the forest."

The hunters thought they saw the huge antelope the next day as they hunted the forest, and the next day as well. Each time it escaped them. Each night

29

they dragged home with long faces. At the evening
campfire the younger brother found few cheerful
words as he told to the child the tale of the elusive
antelope. But the older brother poked silently at the
glowing embers of the fire and kept his thoughts to
himself.

The next morning, the older brother decided to
take a different route as his younger brother followed
the antelope. Creeping silently from behind, he saw
his wife taking off her disguise, but he remained
hidden while he thought of a plan.

That night, when they all had returned to the
campfire and were eating their meal, the oldest
hunter said to his wife, "Tomorrow we will stay in
camp to make more arrows. Leave the child with us
while you go out to gather berries."

The wife quickly agreed and began humming as she
unrolled the sleeping mats.

In the morning, when the sun had barely topped
the hill, the woman hurried off. As soon as she was
out of sight, the men set to work. Finding two logs,
they laid them on their sleeping mats and covered

them with blankets. Then they took up the antelope hides and horns and went off into the woods. They stopped where the wife came to draw water each day. Here the husband, his child, and his brother each dressed themselves in an antelope disguise and sat down to wait.

In a while, the wife came down the path humming to herself. She bent down to dip her hand into the clear water and, as she reached, she stopped. Mirrored in the water were the images of three antelope. The startled woman pulled back her hand slowly so she would not alarm the animals. She crept away from the water and down the path. When she had put some distance between herself and the antelope, she broke her silence and dashed back to camp calling, "Husband! Husband! Three antelope are grazing near the stream!"

No one moved in the camp, so when the wife saw the blanket-covered logs, she thought the men were still sound asleep. "There is no time!" she whispered to herself. "I'll get those antelope myself and surprise everyone." Snatching a bow and arrows, she ran back down the path.

When she reached the stream again, the excited woman could see antelope horns among the branches of the thicket. But as she crept closer, they began to move away. She raised her bow and placed her arrow. Antelope horns moved, shaking the branches and rustling the leaves. Then they disappeared beyond the thicket.

Through brush and brambles and groves, the woman chased the three antelope with her ready arrows. Out of the forest and over the hill they ran.

Then the woman saw that each antelope lacked two legs.

Her excitement dropped like a falling rock. She stopped, but only for an instant. With a screech of anger, the wife bolted forward again and disappeared over the hill in pursuit, legs pounding, shouts flying.

On some clear nights, three stars in a row with a fourth following can be seen crossing the heavens. These, say the ancients, are the two brothers and the child, with the wife still chasing them. They ran so hard, it is told, that they ran right into the sky.

The Spirit of the Snow Goose

During its migrations, the beautiful white snow goose flies over Coeur d'Alene Lake in western Idaho. Some say this was the large bird the Coeur d'Alene Salishans told about in their tales long ago.

For many centuries, people all over the world have seen the outline of a wide-winged bird among the stars. It seems to follow the path of the Milky Way. Many people called this constellation The Swan.

THE SPIRIT OF THE SNOW GOOSE

The Swan

In the cool shadows of a forest long forgotten, there was a clear lake whose deep waters mirrored the clouds by day and the stars by night. It was the resting spot of many creatures of the air. The loon, the blue-winged teal, and the mallard all found their way here. They would float with the clouds across the dark surface. They found rest in the trees rimming the lake and food in the waters.

One evening, three hunters came along a path which wound its way to the lake. They crept softly over the carpet of pine needles. They made no sound as they climbed over rocks. Finally, as the sun was sinking in the West, the three parted the thick branches of the green firs and peered across the waters. There they saw a splendid snow goose floating in the last light of day.

One of the hunters reached for his arrow. His friends stilled his hand. "This noble bird should not be robbed of its life," they said. But the hunter protested. The snow goose would be a great prize to take back to the village.

As they argued, the snow goose lifted its body. It

spread its wings to take flight. The impatient hunter, fearing the great white bird would get away, raised his bow and shot the snow goose. Drawing out its wings to their full span, the beautiful bird dropped to the lake. Then, as the last rays of sunset faded into night, it vanished in the deep, dark waters.

The three hunters stood as though frozen while a strange sadness filled the silence of the forest. Over the lake every last ripple smoothed itself.

Then, as the stars came out and were reflected in the waters, the waiting hunters saw the outline of a great bird take shape. They knew it was the spirit of the snow goose rising to the heavens. It still flies across the night sky, spreading its great wings across the waters of peaceful lakes.

The Tale of the Hungry Skunk

The Salish had many lively sky tales. In one tale, they said it was Coyote who was given the task of carrying the Moon across the sky each night. But as he traveled, they said, Coyote shouted gossip about all the people he saw below. The people were angry and took Coyote's job away.

The imaginative Salish saw another sky story in the constellations of Auriga and Perseus. This one was about a skunk and some women who were cooking camas roots for dinner. The camas root was a form of lily that was excellent eating and plentiful in many places in the high plateau country of Oregon, Washington, and Idaho where the Salish lived.

THE TALE OF THE HUNGRY SKUNK

Auriga, Perseus

Once, when darkness was marching across the sky, the women of the sky country were hurrying about the heavens preparing the evening meal. The men, who were sky fishermen, would be returning home soon and would be hungry.

The women had built a large pit where roots had been placed on hot rocks to cook. The roots had begun to steam, sending their fragrance in sweet-smelling clouds about the heavens.

A skunk wandered from among the trees and caught the scent of the cooking roots. This skunk was a lazy fellow, and it had been a long time since he had found himself a meal. So with his nose twitching and his stomach complaining, Skunk ambled off to see if he could get an easy meal.

It wasn't long before his nose led him to the edge of the village where every woman busied herself with some task. Past the lodges wandered the skunk, past babies sleeping in their cradles. At last Skunk saw the great cooking pit where even now more tender roots were being placed among the hot rocks to steam.

Skunk's stomach growled. He straightened himself

and began to march right up to the oven's circle. "I'm going to take my share of this tasty meal right now!" he said to himself.

"Mother, what is that animal walking toward us?" asked one of the small children helping at the pit.

"Aiiieeeee!" screamed the woman, snatching her child and running away.

"Aiiieeeee!" screeched the other women when they saw what had startled her. At once the place was in an uproar. Skunk marched right on.

But some of the women stayed at the pit. "Come away! Skunk will make you smell like rotten turnips!" cried one of their friends from her doorway.

"No skunk is going to steal my dinner," called back one stubborn woman from the pit. "I don't care how I smell!"

"You're not going to ruin my hard work!" shouted another to Skunk, who had stopped and was thinking about what he might do next.

Running back from their lodges, some of the women joined the others at the pit. There they clustered to protect their meal, sending threatening looks in Skunk's direction.

Skunk was amazed. He had never encountered anyone stubborn enough to challenge him. He looked at the women standing like great rocks around the steaming pit. "Maybe if I am quiet, they will grow tired and forget me," he thought. So he stood very still and waited.

The stubborn women would never give up. They are clustered to this day around their cooking pit. And just a few paces away stands the outline of Skunk, waiting even now for a chance to snatch an easy meal.

The Giant Elk Skin

Cassiopeia's Chair looks like a giant W near the Milky Way. The Inuit saw this constellation as steps cut in the heavenly snows linking the sky country to earth. The Hoh and Quileute, who lived on the Olympic Peninsula of Washington, had a different idea. They were hunters and fishermen. Their tales tell about noble hunters whose arrows and hunting spears sometimes had spiritual powers and about super-animals of fearsome size and speed. These Northwest Coast Indians lived in a mild climate where food from both land and sea was plentiful, so their creativity spilled into all the arts. They wove elaborate blankets, built strong decorated wood houses, carved everyday tools into works of art, and spun tales of high adventure around their mythical heroes.

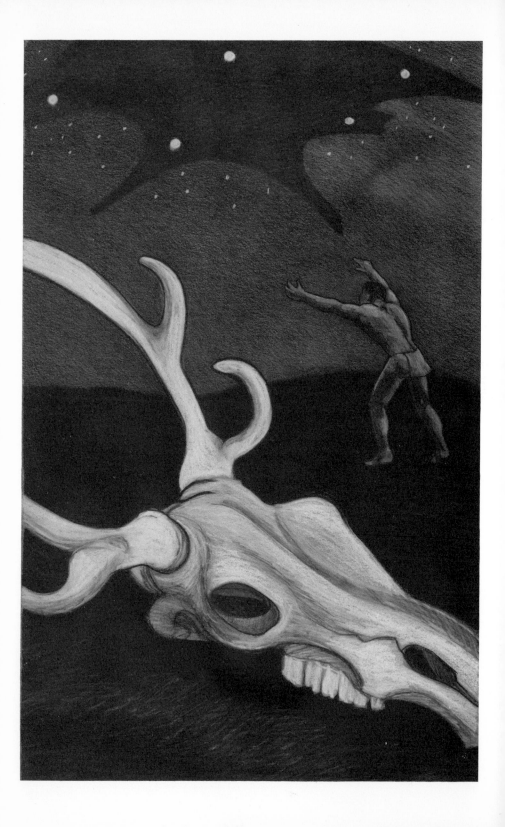

THE GIANT ELK SKIN

Cassiopeia

Long ago five brothers lived along a river. One day four of the brothers went out in their canoe to hunt and fish. When they came to a fork in the river, they pulled up and jumped out to see what hunting might bring them. They hadn't been hunting long when they met a lone man walking across the prairie. He asked what they were doing. When the brothers explained they were hunting for elk, the man said he knew where there was a large herd grazing. "If you will wait here," the man of the prairie said, "I will go ahead and chase the elk in your direction." The brothers all nodded their heads excitedly.

"But look," the man said, "my arrows are much better than yours. They have good medicine." Then he tricked them into trading their arrows for his, which in truth were worthless.

After the man of the prairie left, he changed himself into a giant elk. Then he thundered back to charge the brothers, killing all four of them. Their useless arrows had flown like straw in the wind against the hide of the huge animal.

When the four brothers failed to return, the fifth,

who was the youngest, set out to look for them. Reaching the fork in the river, he came upon their empty canoe and followed the footprints into the tall grass. Soon he too met up with the lone man of the prairie.

The man tried to trick the youngest brother as well, but the brother's guardian spirit was with him. He wasn't so easily fooled. "I trust the good medicine of my own arrows, for I made them with my own hands," he told the lone man.

When the brother refused to trade arrows, the man of the prairie walked on and out of sight. Soon the giant elk came charging after the fifth brother. With his own strong yew arrows, the brother shot the elk and it lay like a mountain on the prairie grass. "This mighty elk will feed many mouths," said the brother to himself. So he set to work preparing the elk meat to take home.

The youngest brother worked through the afternoon sun and into dusk. When he had finished, he began stretching the skin to dry it. "This great hide will have many uses," he thought. But as he struggled to stretch the huge skin, he found it was bigger than the whole prairie. He took the skin, gave a shout, and heaved the great skin into the sky. It is hanging there still. Stars shine, they say, in the holes where the youngest brother had driven stakes to stretch the skin.

As for the brother, he went home and, with his fine yew arrows, was never hungry.

The Birds of Summer

Some Native American legends say there was a time in which animals and humans lived, worked, and talked together. To the Ojibwas and other Algonkians, humans were one kind of "people" and animals were other kinds of "people." In an Ojibwa story about the Big Dipper, it is sometimes hard to guess which is which.

The Ojibwas tell us it is Fisher we see in the group of stars now called the Big Dipper. The Fisher is a lesser-known animal rather like a large mink. It is a cunning hunter and fierce fighter. The handle of the Big Dipper, the Ojibwas said, is Fisher's long, bushy tail.

THE BIRDS OF SUMMER

Big Dipper

It was the snow-swept time long ago when winter seemed never to end. All the people searched the land for some sign that the cold was melting, for summer's turn had arrived. But summer did not come.

As one day blew over the next, the anxious people wondered what to do and called a meeting. Huddled by the lodge fire, Fox, Muskrat, Beaver, and all the brothers of the tribe sat silently. They called upon the spirit of the animal whose name they had been given to help them find a solution. It was finally a cunning hunter named Fisher who spoke first. "Summer has not come because the birds of summer haven't returned," said Fisher, who had traveled many distant hills.

"What could have happened?" the people wondered. They talked about how the birds left each year as the trees turned golden.

"Never have the birds failed to return," said the most ancient of the elders.

While the people talked, Fisher was thinking. "I think I know who might be holding back the birds of summer," Fisher said shortly. "I have a selfish cousin

who wants all good things for himself. He has been
named Cruel-Face. If he has captured the birds of
summer, he will keep them."

With angry cries the people asked Fisher what they
could do.

"This Cruel-Face has the will of a grizzly bear,"
Fisher answered. "But the bowl he fills for himself
spills into the hands of his followers. To keep their
comforts, his people jump to every command of this
man-without-a-heart."

Fisher looked slowly around the campfire at the
faces of Beaver, Caribou, Fox, and the others. "Pre-
pare for a journey of ten sleeps," he said. "We must
go to Cruel-Face to bring back the birds of summer."

The people agreed and parted to gather their
things. In the morning Fisher lead his people out of
camp and across the wind-swept fields.

They traveled through groves of barren trees. They
walked along snow-blanketed game trails. They struggled through snow drifts and over frozen rivers. On
the eighth day, cold still swept the ragged path. On
every side, the world stretched grey and lifeless.
Fisher told them to make camp for the night and to

look into the campfire for visions of a warm and sunny day. But some of the travelers mumbled about turning back.

The next morning, as they walked, the air began to feel warmer. The snow melted into the path and streams gurgled. By evening the travelers had removed their heavy robes. They came upon a wide, clear lake and laid down their packs in the sweet-smelling grass along the shore. It felt like spring.

When the people wondered at this change, Fisher pointed to the light of campfires across the lake. "That is the village of Cruel-Face. Warm breezes blow here because the birds of summer have never left this place," he said. "I will find Cruel-Face but you must help."

Then Fisher worked out a plan. Muskrat and Beaver were to start first before dawn. It was their job to make holes in the villagers' canoes and weaken their paddles. "When light begins to break," he said to Caribou, "you must swim into the lake. Fox will make barking noises to signal Caribou's crossing," he continued. "The rest of you must set up a commotion that all the world will hear." Fisher thought for a moment, then he added, "There is one more thing. If the birds of summer come along, don't wait for me. Follow them!"

"We won't go without you," cried Caribou, "no matter what happens."

But Fisher silenced Caribou. "No, my friend, whatever happens, we must release the birds of summer. Their spirits cry out to travel their own path."

"We will see that nothing stops them!" Caribou said, and everyone agreed.

When dawn came, Fox's barking awakened Cruel-Face's people. Creeping from their lodges to see what the noise was about, they saw Caribou jumping into the lake. The eager villagers raced to their canoes with their bows and arrows. Caribou swam farther into the deep waters until only his shining antlers could be seen from the shore.

Fisher, hiding in the brush, watched the villagers hurrying off. Then he stole to the lodge of their chief.

He found Cruel-Face seated before a small fire in the center of his earthen floor. A collection of arrow shafts was at his side. All around him, filling the lodge from floor to ceiling, were stacks and stacks of birchbark boxes.

The bullish chief hunched toward the fire, using a long stick to jab again and again into a small heating pot resting on glowing logs. The pot held warm sturgeon glue which Cruel-Face was using to join feathers to arrow shafts.

Fisher saw that Cruel-Face was too busy making his arrows to notice him. Fisher peered through the smoky air and he listened. Then he crept toward the boxes.

Cruel-Face suddenly was on him like a snarling

wolf. But Fisher was quick. Snatching the glue stick from Cruel-Face's grasp, Fisher swished the dripping stick around, swabbing the mouth of the chief with a thick stroke of warm glue.

The astonished chief's hands shot to his face, where they stuck like a leech sticks to bare skin. He leaped up to cry out, but no cry came. His mouth was glued tight. Cruel-Face hopped around the lodge. Feathers flew. Boxes crashed. Sticks scattered.

The agile Fisher wasted no time. He dashed among the boxes, opening one, poking a hole in another. It was just as he had suspected. From the first box flew the thrushes and the warblers. From the second came finches and sparrows. Then came jays and wrens, swallows, woodpeckers, and bluebirds.

As his cousin thrashed about the lodge, Fisher opened every box. A rainbow cloud of birds rose from the lodge of the selfish chief. Like smoke it drifted out and over the lake where the people of Cruel-Face in their leaky canoes looked up.

"Look!" cried a warrior.

"Listen!" called others. "The birds of summer are getting away!" They began to whip their canoes around toward the village. Their paddles, damaged by Muskrat and Beaver, broke against the urgent strokes of the villagers. The canoes took on water and sank. Soon the people of Cruel-Face were swimming for shore.

As the birds of summer flew across the lake and over the forests, Fox, Caribou, Muskrat, Beaver, and all of Fisher's friends followed in great haste. Behind them a winter wind was already swirling around the lodges.

As for Fisher, he was still dodging the thrashings of

the angry chief, but one small box remained to be opened. Using an arrow shaft, Fisher poked a hole in the box and out darted a flurry of hummingbirds. They flashed and whirred around the head of Cruel-Face while Fisher dashed out of the lodge.

As a rabbit runs before the fox, Fisher ran from the chief to join his friends. He ran through the village, past the lodges, and smack into the raging mob of cold, wet villagers emerging from the lake.

Like an animal cornered, Fisher crouched, looking for an escape. Then he sprang for a tall tree. Climbing furiously, Fisher heard the panting of the angry villagers behind him. The tree shook. Branches snapped. Beyond him stretched only the sky.

"Brave Fisher!" whispered the stars. "Brave Fisher, you are our brother." Their voices called like the song of a hundred birds. Fisher thrust out his arms. Then, tearing from the grasp of the people, rising over treetops and hills, Fisher joined the friendly stars in the winter sky.

Beaver, Caribou, Fox, and the rest of the travelers returned to their village with the birds of summer. Before them, all the way, flowers bloomed and sleeping buds unfolded. But fear froze their hearts when the people thought about what might have happened to Fisher. After only one night, they set upon the path again to find their friend who had not returned.

The moon wasted from bright fullness to a thin sliver while Fisher's people searched for him. One night the people had gathered around the campfire when one small boy pointed to the sky. "I see Fisher there among the stars!" he said.

The people looked. Then they looked again. "Brave

Fisher has escaped to the sky country!" they murmured excitedly one to the other. Then they hurried to tell the story of Fisher and the birds of summer to all the people of the village.

"We will keep those birds of summer for ourselves from this day on," some of the villagers cried when they heard the story. "We can make sure the warm winds of summer always blow across our land."

But others looked up at the sky and asked, "What would Fisher say about this?"

"Fisher would say the birds of summer should be free to be themselves," said Fox, and many agreed.

That is why things are as they are. For half of the year the people walk lightly in warm breezes. They smell the fragrance of a thousand flowers and work to the song of the meadowlark. But when the traveling moon appears in the heavens, the birds of summer take wing. Cold winds blow. The sun sinks lower in the sky and snow sweeps the path. Then the people search the winter sky for Fisher and make the long nights pass more quickly sharing stories about their brave friend and the birds of summer.

The Never-Ending Bear Hunt

The stars in the sky seem to revolve around the North Star, also called Polaris, during the night. The sky appears to change as the night moves on, but it also changes throughout the year. The two constellations of Bootes and Corona Borealis seem to sink so low in the night sky that they disappear below the horizon and aren't seen for several months of the year. At the same time, the Big Dipper is visible all year long but looks like it is standing upright during some months and upside down in others. Stars don't really move, but they appear to because the earth spins on its axis.

The Micmac Indians of Nova Scotia told a story to fit the changing look of the starry sky. It is a story that never ends.

THE NEVER-ENDING BEAR HUNT

The Big Dipper
Bootes
Corona Borealis

Far away in the sky country, a bear woke up from a
long winter sleep. She left her rocky den on the hill
and lumbered off to search for berries. A sharp-eyed
chickadee, flitting around the bushes, saw the bear
and flew off to call his friends around him.

"It has been a long winter and I am hungry," said
Chickadee. "I am going bear hunting. Who will come
with me?"

Six of his friends agreed to join Chickadee, and at
once they set out to find the bear.

Chickadee was the smallest hunter, but he was also
the wisest. He carried along a pot for boiling his
dinner. Robin, who was larger, was called upon to
lead the hunting party. Moose-bird was impatient and
took his place behind Chickadee. He intended to help
himself to Chickadee's pot. Pigeon, Blue Jay, Horned
Owl and Saw-whet all fell into place behind Moose-
bird as the party started out.

Since food had been scarce through the winter, the
hunters hurried to track their dinner. They found,
though, that large and awkward as she seemed, Bear

could move quite fast. The hunters were not catching up with her.

All summer the bear moved across the land of the stars while the hungry hunters followed. As autumn approached, some of them grew too weary to continue.

"I'm too far behind to catch up," said Saw-whet at the very end of the line. He was a clumsy owl and heavier than the others. Saw-whet dropped out of the chase first.

"Where's that lazy Saw-whet?" fretted Horned Owl, and he left to find his cousin.

Blue Jay tried to stay in the hunt, but by-and-by he and Pigeon lost their way and fell out of sight. That left only Robin, Chickadee with his pot, and Moose-bird to follow the trail of the bear.

At last, deep into autumn, the hunters overtook their prey. The cornered bear reared up on her hind legs and tried to defend herself. Growling and clawing she stood, but Robin shot her with his arrow. The bear fell over on her back, her blood coloring the leaves of autumn and staining Robin's breast a brilliant red.

All during the winter the dead bear lay on her back in the sky country. But that was not the end of the story. Her life spirit had entered another bear who had found its way to the den and was fast asleep. When spring awakens the sleeping earth, the den will reappear. A new star bear will come out of the den to search for berries in the sky, and Chickadee will begin the hunt again, as he does every year.

Moon and His Sister

Some of the greatest parties of all times were thrown by the Indians of the Northwest Coast. These tremendous give-away feasts were called potlatches. It was a contest to see which party would lavish the most food and the most extravagant gifts on its guests. A potlatch was an occasion for storytelling contests, too. Families had their own tales and sometimes acted them out with costumes and elaborate masks carved from wood. Moon masks were round and often decorated with pearly white shells. The Thompson River Indians who lived on the plateaus of south-central British Columbia shared the potlatch custom. They had a tale of a good-natured moon. Some families said his sister was a frog, others a rabbit. In this tale she is just a girl carrying water buckets.

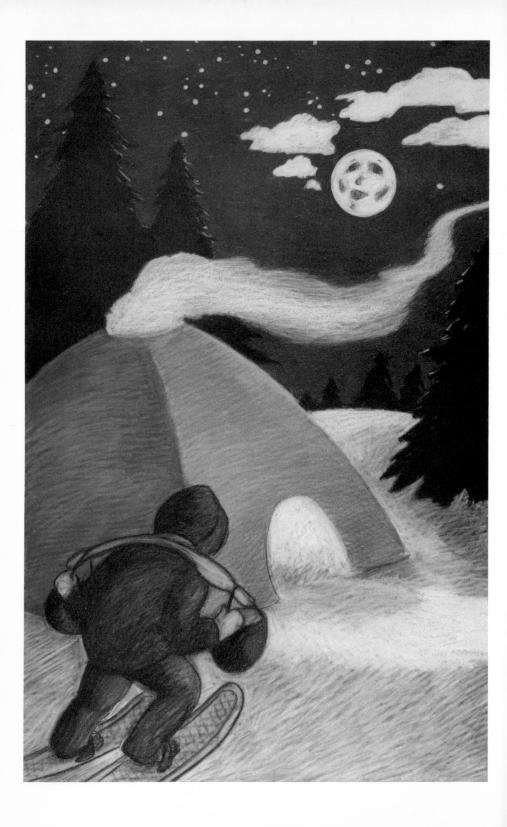

MOON AND HIS SISTER

Small Star Near the Moon

The Moon was once a merry Indian whose face was even more brilliant than the Sun. He had one sister, a small star who could often be seen trailing along beside him, and countless star friends. One day, Moon called all of his friends together for a great feast. His small house was soon packed with guests.

When his sister arrived, Moon called for her to fetch water for him in her buckets. The task was not easy for deep winter was upon them, but the little sister went anyway. The cold wind howled. Ice had to be chipped from the water source, and the buckets were as heavy as great rocks.

When Moon's weary sister returned, there was hardly room in the crowded house for her to put down the buckets. She called to her brother. "Where can I sit?"

Moon's merry face burst into a grin. "There isn't space left for even a mouse in here," he laughed. "I guess you'll just have to sit on my head."

Moon's little sister was in no mood for his jokes. At once she jumped onto his head, and there she sits today with her water buckets. It is her shadow that dims his face.

Someday Moon hopes to shine as bright as the sun again. But he is a patient fellow. He enjoys smoking his pipe while he waits for his sister to move. On many nights cloud puffs from his pipe float about the sky.

Moon's star guests had such a good time at his party that they left the party in groups and danced their way across the sky. Most of them are there still, dancing and talking to one another.

The Boy Who Shot the Star to Find His Friend

The moon is a kind but powerful woman in many Native American Indian stories. In one tale she rescues a freezing girl from her cruel stepmother by helping her escape to the sky. But the Tlingits of the Alaskan panhandle told a story of an angry moon bent on revenge and of a star that promised help.

To many of the Northern tribes, the sky was like a roof through which the shining faces or homes of the star people would shine on those below. Some, like the Blackfoot Indians, thought stars were grandparents or relatives who had died but continued to love and be concerned for their earthly relatives.

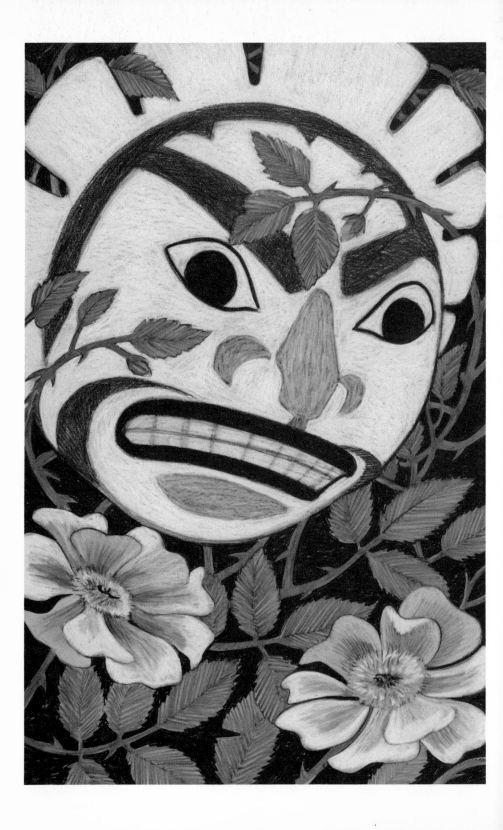

THE BOY WHO SHOT THE STAR TO FIND HIS FRIEND

Star Near the Moon

A hunter's son and the son of a chief were once close friends. The boys played often on a hill beyond the village where they made arrows and practiced shooting them.

One night, as they climbed to the top of the hill, the hunter's son looked at the star-filled sky and remarked, "How small and weak the moon looks tonight." The chief's son warned him that he must not make the moon angry, but it was too late. The moon had heard the remark and was angry.

Suddenly a light like a rainbow surrounded the boys. When it disappeared, the chief's son was alone on the hill. He knew the angry moon had taken his friend.

The chief's son did not know what to do. He began shooting arrows, thinking he might try to hit the star closest to the moon. When he had used up all his arrows, he fell asleep, sad and exhausted.

The chief's son could not believe what he saw when he opened his eyes. There, hanging from the sky was a ladder of arrows! He had no idea what the ladder meant, but on the chance that it might have something to do with the disappearance of his friend, the boy began to climb. The ladder took him beyond the bushes and treetops and into the clouds. He climbed for three days and nights. When he was hungry, he ate fruit from the twigs and branches caught in his hair. Reaching the top of the ladder at last, the boy fell asleep, exhausted again.

"Wake up! Wake up!" the boy heard through his sleep. "We know why you are here!" A young girl was shaking the shoulder of the chief's son. When he was awake, the girl led him to her grandmother's house. "We looked for you after your arrows hit our house," said the girl.

The grandmother welcomed the chief's son and told him that his friend was a captive in the moon's house next door. "We've heard him wailing for three days," she said. "We will do what we can to help you." With that, the old woman handed the boy three objects—a spruce cone, a rose branch, and a rock. "You will know when to make good use of these," she said.

The chief's son hurried to Moon's house and untied his friend. Climbing to the roof, he placed the spruce cone in the smoke hole of the house. "The wind will whistle through the cone and set up a wailing," whispered the boy to his friend. Then the two ran as fast as they could away from the Moon's house.

Moon wasn't fooled long by the howling cone. He came rolling after the boys faster than they could run. When Moon was at their heels, the chief's son tossed back the rose branch. It burst into a tangle of vines and thorns. While the moon struggled to free himself, the boys ran ahead.

"You'll be sorry you tricked the moon!" roared Moon as he rumbled down upon them again. "I'll make you both prisoners!"

The chief's son looked over his shoulder and saw the moon reaching for him. He threw the rock. Crash! The rock became a mountain, and Moon ran right into it.

The boys puffed and panted back to the safety of the old grandmother's house. Now they wanted only to leave the sky country and go back home. The kind old grandmother knew what they were thinking. "Lie down here and rest," she told them. "Think of nothing but the hill where you played with your arrows. Everything will be as it should."

By now the boys knew how wise the old woman was, so they did exactly as she ordered. Curling up, they fell fast asleep at her feet.

When they awakened, the two friends found themselves lying on their grassy hilltop. Shaking sleep from their heads and twigs from their clothes, they walked back to their village. Their families, who had thought they would never see them again, held a great feast to celebrate their return.

Now when the two friends sit on their hill, they send thanks to the star next to the moon, for they know it is the small house of the grandmother who saved them from the angry moon.

The Dancing Braves

Pleiades is a small but brilliant cluster which seems to have seven stars. There are really many less visible stars in this shimmering constellation. It inspired tale-tellers across the continent. To some it was a swarm of bees. The Cherokees said Pleiades was seven boys who ran away from home. They were angry because their mothers gave them soup boiled from sticks and stones as punishment for not doing their work.

The Iroquois Indians, who lived in the woodlands of New York State, believed in witchcraft. Their tale about Pleiades has the spooky touch of curses and bewitchment.

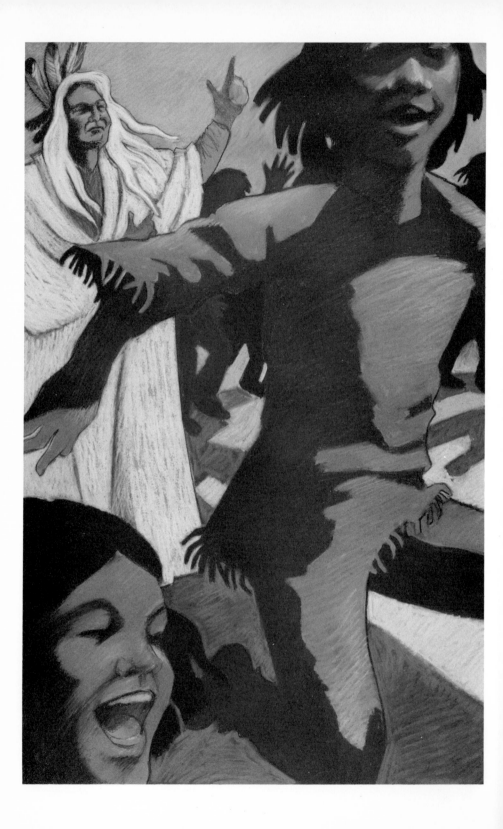

THE DANCING BRAVES

Pleiades

Once long ago when summer was fading and the people of the tribe were building winter lodges, some of the younger boys played together near the edge of the woods. Too young to join the men hunting for winter meat, they pretended to be great warriors and danced the war dances.

One afternoon a strange old man appeared to the boys as they danced. He was dressed in a startling way. White feathers covered his robes, and his hair hung long and silver. Perhaps the stranger was one of the grandparents of the sky country. Perhaps he was only a confused old man. Whatever he may have been, his strong words were a warning to the boys that their wild dancing would come to no good. The boys paid no attention but went right on with their dances.

The next day they gathered again and danced until their shadows were longer than they were. Now the braves were hungry and tired but, when they thought of resting, they couldn't seem to stop. Their feet seemed to keep time to some mysterious beat that whirled and twirled them around their circle. Indeed, their feet seemed hardly to touch the ground. When they looked, the boys saw that they were rising in the air over rocks and bushes and trees.

Below, some of the tribe members saw the dancing braves. "Come back!" they pleaded.

"Stop dancing!" demanded the chief.

But still the boys rose dancing in the air.

The noise of the shouting reached the setting sun. He tried to stop the boys, but he had sunk too low in the heavens. The braves danced past, and the sun fell behind the hills.

Now Moon came up and wondered what the commotion was all about. The dancing braves shouted and whooped as they danced around her. "Stop!" she commanded in a voice that thundered.

"We cannot," cried the braves. So Moon invited them to join her legions of stars marching across the sky. Bouncing and whooping, the boys twirled into the procession, and soon all of the stars were whirling. The sky was in a flurry. Moon was alarmed.

"I must bring peace to the heavens and rest to these boys," Moon thought to herself. And after thinking a moment longer, Moon transformed the braves into a group of stars, placing them near the top of the sky.

Moon, in her wisdom, decided the boys should preside over the Indian New Year. Their path in the heavens brings them to stand each year directly over the Council House during the New Year's feast. Then, as Indians watch, the light of these small, bright stars sparkles and dances in the sky and everyone remembers the Dancing Braves.

The Maidens of the Northern Crown

There is an incomplete circle of stars in the sky called the Northern Crown. Indian storytellers wondered why a star seemed to be missing. No one knows who told this story first, but the bittersweet tale was shared with different twists across the land. It came to be one of the most beloved of all Indian legends. Among the gentle hills and cool forests of the northern Great Lakes country, the Ojibwas told their version. The hunter heroes of their tales were able to change themselves into other forms as they wished, so this hunter became a mouse.

THE MAIDENS OF THE NORTHERN CROWN

Northern Crown

Once in a time long before this one, a young hunter returning to his village paused in a clearing. He had come upon a strange circle path. He searched but could find no path leading up to or away from the circle in the field. Shaking his head with bewilderment, he crouched down to wait and watch from the shadows of a birch grove. When night had fallen, the hunter heard strange music and noticed that a cluster of stars in the sky seemed to be traveling toward him. He clutched his arrows and caught his breath as the star cluster alighted in the clearing.

"I must be dreaming," murmured the hunter as he watched twelve beautiful maidens climb from a basket and begin to dance around the circle. They must have come here often, the hunter thought, because they wasted no time and seemed to know the place. When he had shaken the wonder from his head, the hunter stepped out of the shadows toward the dancing maidens. The music and the dancing stopped at once. Like birds seeking the safety of their nest, the maidens flew to their star basket. It rose at once into the night the way it had come.

The hunter, determined to find out what or whom he had seen, returned to the clearing on the following evening. Everything happened just as before. This time though, the hunter waited for a while and watched before cautiously letting himself be seen. The maidens ran from him again and disappeared into their basket. But the hunter had seen something that made him more determined than before. Among the maidens was one who was more graceful and, to the hunter's eyes, more beautiful than any of the others. "I must know this maiden," said the hunter to himself. And so he prepared to come again.

On the third night, the hunter changed himself into a mouse and hid in the grasses. The basket came down as it had before. This time, one dance flowed into the other, and the maidens stayed in the clearing until the stars had traveled from one horizon to the other.

Among the grass blades and stems, the mouse/hunter watched. And as he watched, he inched his way forward. It was the youngest dancing maid who had caught his eye, and now his heart pounded for her as he crept to her very feet. Suddenly then, the music came to an end and the maidens turned to their basket. Springing forward, the mouse/hunter became himself again and, with arms outreached, he grasped the youngest maid. The maidens cried out for their youngest sister, and she thrust her graceful body against the arms that held her fast. But the basket flew from the field and vanished.

Because he was kind and good, in time the hunter won the heart of the star maiden, and she became his wife. In a little more time, they had a son. As the child grew and the family worked and played together, the star woman was happy.

The hunter's wife was from the land of the star people, though, and could not live on earth forever. One night, while the hunter and his son slept, the eleven sisters came in their basket and carried the youngest sister off to the sky. The star people were pleased to have the circle of dancing sisters complete again, but they worried about the youngest sister, who never smiled. Although she loved her sisters, the hunter's wife was lonely and wept for her lost family.

At last the star people took pity on the youngest sister. They brought the hunter and his son to visit the star woman, but for only one night. "These are earth creatures," warned the father of the star people. "They must return or they will die."

"We will make the most of our time together," said the hunter's wife, and they did.

The star people watched the family and were moved. They wanted to help, so the father of the star people agreed to change the star wife, the hunter, and their son into three white falcons. Now the three belong to neither sky nor earth. They are free to visit both as they please. The remaining maidens of the Northern Crown dance together still. But it is said they will never leave the sky again.

The last star to disappear just before sunrise is the Morning Star. Although North American Indians did not know that this was really a planet and not a star, they did notice that it had no fixed position among the constellations. Their tales often made the roaming Morning Star a noble hunter. Morning Star and all the other star people were said to be super-human with powers only imagined by earthlings. The Blackfoot Indians allowed humans to marry stars in their tales. The lives of these humans were always tangled when they failed to understand the ways of the star people.

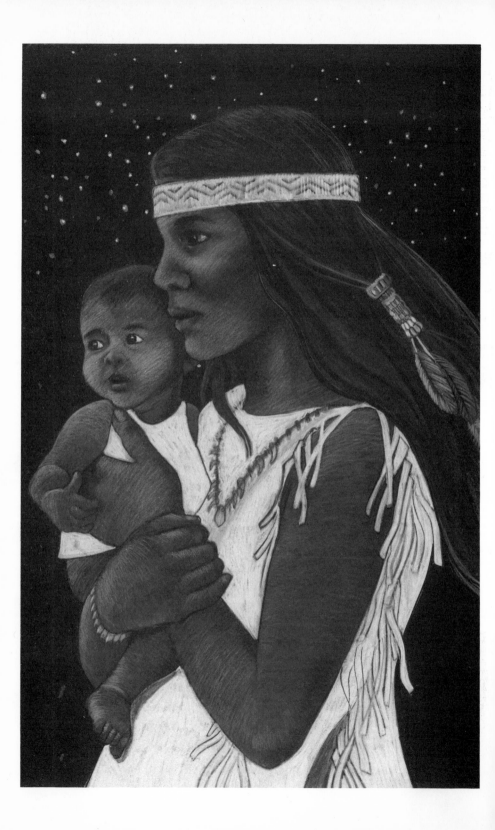

MORNING STAR TAKES A WIFE

Morning Star
Polaris

One hot summer night, when the world was young and strange things were possible, two maidens decided to sleep outside. As they drifted in and out of sleep, they watched the stars and, as maidens do, they dreamed about the husbands they might have one day. "I would have a hunter who keeps meat on the campfire and soft skins in our lodge," sighed one of the maids.

The other shook her head. "Whatever the wind brings me I would take if only he were bold in spirit." Then she pointed to the sky. "See that star there, the bright one? I want that one for a husband." Laughing, she rolled over, and they both fell asleep again.

The next day, as this impulsive maiden was gathering firewood in the forest, a handsome stranger came up to her. "I am the star man you wished for," he told the surprised young woman. "My name is Morning Star, and I have come for you."

The maiden took a half step away. She looked and thought, thought and looked. This handsome young man wore a generous robe of thick beaver skins and in his hair hung an eagle plume. "He has the walk of a man of importance," observed the girl to herself. "Yet, there is a merry look in his eye." So with a toss of her head, she consented to go away with him.

"Look one last time down the footpath winding to your village," Morning Star said, pointing. "You cannot look back again." Morning Star watched as the maiden with a mind of her own gave but a glance over her shoulder. "Now you must shut your eyes," he commanded, placing an eagle plume in her hair, "and never look down." Then he took her boldly and led her to the sky. The laughter they shared fell like soft rain on the empty footpath.

Morning Star took his bride first to visit his mother, Moon, and his father, Sun. To welcome her to their lodge, Moon and Sun gave the young woman four berries and a few drops of water in a shell. Although she ate and ate, Morning Star's bride could not finish the berries or sip the last drop of water. There seemed always to be more. Then Moon offered another gift to Morning Star's bride with these words: "This," she said, "is a digger which you may use to dig roots for cooking any place in our land but one." Then

Moon pointed across the gardens of the sky to a large turnip. "That turnip is a sacred root to the sky people and must never be uprooted," she commanded.

"I will not fail to honor your turnip," promised the young woman as she hurried off with her handsome husband.

Morning Star and his bride were a contented pair, and in good time they had a child. In all the heavens there was nothing the star wife needed. Yet, although she was happy, she wondered about the sacred turnip. "Moon's rule is foolish," she thought. Her curiosity nagged at her as a fly nags on a hot summer day.

Finally, the nagging buzzed louder than the whisper of her pledge. "The sky country is full of turnips," she muttered to herself. "Who will know if I dig that one up?" So while her baby played near her, Morning Star's Wife dug up the forbidden root.

That evening, Moon shouted at Morning Star's door. "What have you done with the sacred turnip?" Moon demanded of the earthly wife. No truth could be hidden from Moon. Morning Star's Wife could only confess what she had done.

The lodge was darkly silent. "What did you see when you dug out the turnip?" asked Moon.

The wife of Morning Star replied, "I looked down through the hole and saw the earth, the trees, the rivers, and the lodges of my people."

Moon scowled. Sun's face clouded. The merry look faded from Morning Star's eyes. "I warned you never to look back," he said. "Now I cannot keep you with me any longer. You must take the boy with you and go back to your people."

Sun went to Spider to ask him to spin a strong web. In this, the star man's wife would be lowered to earth again. When Spider had done his work, Sun spoke again to the wife. "You have taken the law of the sky people carelessly," he frowned. "Now I have another rule you must follow." Then he told her she would be allowed to keep her son with her only if she followed his command. "When you reach the lodges of your people, you must not let the boy touch earth for fourteen days. If he does, he will be returned at once to the land of the stars," Sun said like a bear growls warning.

With Sun's words heavy in her thoughts, Morning Star's Wife was lowered with her child through the turnip hole to earth.

The people of Morning Star's Wife welcomed her back with a feast that lasted three days, for they had been sure she was dead. The woman ate and danced with the others, but she watched her small son every moment. Never would she let him slide to the ground as he begged. Never could he play in the dirt. Sun's warning echoed in her head!

"She loves her son more than life itself," whispered

the women of the village.

"She worries foolishly," scolded the star wife's old mother.

But one day Morning Star's Wife needed water for cooking. It was quiet in the lodge, and her son slept soundly on his bed. "What harm can come while my son sleeps so deeply?" thought Morning Star's Wife. "I will be out of the lodge and back again in the flash of a falling star." So, as she hurried off with her water bucket, she called to her mother, "Watch him carefully so that he stays on the bed!"

The old mother settled herself beside her grandson's bed, but soon the warmth of the darkened lodge closed around her. "My daughter worries foolishly," she muttered and allowed herself to fall asleep. Before long her rumbling snores had stirred the child beside her. He opened his eyes. He stretched his legs to the edge of the bed. Then he crawled down to play in the dirt, laughing to be free at last.

Like a leaf caught in the wind, when his toes grazed the earthen floor, the child rose to the top of the lodge. Out the smoke hole, above the trees he blew, over the hills and into the sky.

Slivers of baby laughter fell on the ears of the star wife returning with her water. Dropping the bucket, she flew into the lodge, shouting her son's name. But the bed and the room stood empty of her small son's form.

That night, wrapped in her sadness, Morning Star's Wife lay under clear skies searching the heavens for some sign of her lost child. Her eyes swept and swept again the farthest reaches of the sky and, when her head ached from the watching, she was sure she saw something different. A new star gleamed where the empty turnip hole had once been. Morning Star's Wife kept her eyes on the star all night. She watched it the next night and the next. This star seemed easy to find. It kept its place always in the sky while the other stars revolved around it. In time Morning Star's Wife looked upon this star as her own.

Among the people of Morning Star's Wife, her star became known as the Fixed Star. They used it to help them tell direction. They looked for it to help them chart the heavens. But to Morning Star's Wife, the Fixed Star brought a special comfort. When she was lonely, she could always find her son. She knew he would look down on her always from his place above.

ONE LAST WORD FROM THE STARS

On warm summer nights when the sky is like dark glass and the stars stand clear enough to count, beware! The Sioux warned against trying to count the stars. It was believed that if you dared to look at the sky and count even "one" mentally, you might be doomed. They thought death was certain if the counting was begun but not finished.

WHERE THE TALES BEGAN

1. ***COYOTE MAKES THE CONSTELLATIONS*** was collected in 1921 by Lucillus V. McWhorter.

2. ***ADVENTURE ALONG THE WHITE RIVER IN THE SKY:*** Dr. Herman Haeberlin heard this story from the Snohomish but died before he was able to publish it. Erna Gunther Spier wrote a version for him in 1924.

3. ***THE RACE FOR THE PRIZE FISH*** was also recorded by Lucillus V. McWhorter, who heard it from the Wascos.

4. ***THE ANTELOPE CHASE*** was told by Tom Austin to Robert H. Lowie who recorded it for the American Folklore Society.

5. ***THE SPIRIT OF THE SNOW GOOSE*** is based on a brief fragment found in the Memoirs of the American Folklore Society, 1917.

6. ***THE TALE OF THE HUNGRY SKUNK*** was crafted from comments written by Franz Boaz in 1917.

7. ***THE GIANT ELK SKIN*** is based on parts of a story recorded in 1909 by L.V.W. Walters.

8. ***THE BIRDS OF SUMMER*** is based on parts of a story recorded in 1919 by William Jones.

9. ***THE NEVER-ENDING BEAR HUNT*** was carefully recorded with drawings by Stansbury Hagar in 1900.

10. **MOON AND HIS SISTER** is based on variants of a widely told tale.

11. **THE BOY WHO SHOT THE STAR TO FIND HIS FRIEND** has been passed to us by the Tlinget peoples. John R. Swanton wrote it down in 1909.

12. **THE DANCING BRAVES** is retold from several versions. One was reported by Wm. M. Beauchamp in 1900.

13. **THE MAIDENS OF THE NORTHERN CROWN** is an old tale with many versions. Henry R. Schoolcraft wrote his in 1860.

14. **MORNING STAR TAKES A WIFE** was adapted from parts of a Blackfeet legend told to Clark Wissler by Wolf-Head, who died in 1905.

The designs and illustrations for this book were carefully researched for each tribe represented, largely through the resources of the Milwaukee Public Museum.

GLOSSARY

Alaskan panhandle—the southward extending Pacific coastline of the state of Alaska

Antelope—the mammal known in North America as the antelope is actually the pronghorn, and is the swiftest of all North American mammals

Arrow shaft—the long stem to which the head and feathers of an arrow are attached

Auriga—constellation also called "The Charioteer", located between Perseus and Gemini

Ax—handled tool with a sharpened end used for chopping

Beaver—a large rodent with a broad, flat tail. With its long front teeth, the beaver cuts trees which it uses to build dams and dens along streams.

Betelgeuse—a very bright star of the first magnitude seen near one shoulder of Orion, the constellation also called "The Hunter"

Big Dipper—the seven most obvious stars (which resemble a dipper) in the constellation Ursa Major or Big Bear.

Big Horn—a wild sheep. The males have large curling horns.

Birchbark boxes—lidded containers made by lacing together strips of bark from the birch tree

Boötes—also known as "The Herdsman." The handle of the Big Dipper points to this constellation.

Camas root—the edible bulb of the camas plant, a member of the lily family

Canoe—a long, narrow boat made of wood, bark or hides. Canoes made from birchbark were lightweight and easy for one or a few to carry. Some dugout canoes, made from huge logs, could carry more than fifty people. These were often decorated.

Caribou—a member of the deer family living in northern forests and bogs. Unlike other deer, both males and females have antlers.

Cassiopeia's Chair—a W-shaped constellation located between Andromeda and Cepheus

Chickadee—a small, lively bird with grey back and wings

Chinook wind—along the Pacific coast this is a warm wind which comes from the southwest. When it blows down the mountains in winter and early spring, it often melts snow at the base of the slopes.

Clearing—an area without trees

Constellation—a group of stars which appear to resemble a person or object

Corona Borealis—also known as the Northern Crown, a small constellation which seems to be a broken circle, between Hercules and Boötes

Council house—meeting place for the tribal council

Coyote—a swift, cunning mammal related to, but smaller than, the wolf. There are many American Indian tales about Coyote.

Eagle plume—a cluster of feathers worn as an ornament

Elk—the largest member of the deer family. Older males have large, many-tinted antlers.

Fir—an evergreen of the pine family

Fisher—a dark brown forest mammal related to weasels. Fishers are fierce hunters.

Fixed Star—also known as Polaris or The North Star

Fox—a sly, cunning mammal of the dog family having a bushy tail

Good medicine—helpful spiritual powers

Grazing—to feed on the vegetation

Great White River in the Sky—the name given by some Native Americans to the Milky Way

Grizzly Bear—a large and powerful bear of a brownish-yellow color

Guardian spirit—a supernatural being that was a personal spiritual helper and the source of a man's or a woman's power

High Plateau Country of Oregon—the Columbia plateau covering most of eastern Oregon. Much of this area is rugged and mountainous.

Horizon—the place where earth and sky seem to meet

Horned Owl—a large owl with tufts of feathers resembling horns on either side of its head

Labrador—a large peninsula in northeastern Canada bordered by Hudson Bay and the Atlantic Ocean

Ladle—a utensil used for dipping up liquid

Leech—a segmented worm which usually feeds on blood. Most live in water.

Migrations—the regular journey from one region to another for feeding and breeding

Milky Way—seen as a broad, irregular band of light stretching across the night sky, it is actually the light of billions of stars in our own galaxy

Morning Star—the last star visible in the sky after daybreak. The Morning Star is a planet, not a real star (usually the planet Venus.) Some ancients said Morning Star was a hunter among the sky people.

Mosquitoes—small insects with long legs. The female feeds on the blood of mammals.

Muskrat—mammal about the size of a small house cat which has dense dark brown fur and lives along streams and rivers. Water vegetation is its main food and the building material for its houses.

North Star—also known as *Polaris*. This is the star in the Northern Hemisphere toward which the axis of the earth points. As a result, when we look at the sky, all of the stars seem to circle around this star.

Northwest Coast—an area of the North American Pacific Coast extending northward from Northern California to Alaska

Nova Scotia—includes a peninsula of the Canadian mainland as well as Cape Breton Island and extends into the Atlantic Ocean northeast of Maine

Olympic Peninsula of Washington—a rugged mountain region in the northwest corner of Washington State bordered by the Strait of Juan de Fuca on the north and the Pacific Ocean on the west

Orion—a constellation that represents a hunter with a belt and sword. It is a winter constellation and has more bright stars than any other.

Perseus—a constellation located between Taurus ("The Bull") and Cassiopeia

Planet—one of the large heavenly bodies which revolve around our sun. At night planets reflect the light of our sun and look like stars, but are not. Ancient people noticed that the planets moved on their own individual paths across the heavens.

Pleiades—a bright cluster of stars in the constellation Taurus or "The Bull." Six or seven of the stars are visible to the average eye.

Polaris—another name for the North Star

Potlatch—at these lavish feasts, the host gave away valuable gifts to guests

Prairie—mostly level, grass-covered plains

Puget Sound—a huge bay between the Olympic Peninsula and the Cascade Mountains in Washington State. It is connected to the Pacific Ocean by the Strait of Juan de Fuca.

Robin—a migratory bird commonly known for its red breast

Salmon—a fish. The Pacific Salmon is known for the long journeys it makes upstream to its breeding grounds.

Saw-whet—a small owl with a harsh voice

Skunk—a cat-sized animal which sprays a foul smelling scent when threatened

Smoke hole—an opening constructed in houses, tipis, and lodges so that smoke from the fire could escape

Snow goose—a large bird which breeds in the Artic tundra and winters in more southern marshes

Spruce—an evergreen pine tree

Spruce cone—the pinecone from a spruce tree

Star—a shining heavenly body visible in the sky at night. Our sun is a star.

Sturgeon glue—glue made by cooking the heads, bones, and scales of a fish until a gelatin is formed

Trickster—someone who fools others

Turnip—a vegetable with edible leaves and root

Warrior—a person experienced in fighting wars

Water buckets—containers usually made from carved wood, woven plant material, or tightly sealed birchbark

White falcon—a magnificent long-winged bird

Yew—an evergreen tree or bush